HEIDI HECKELBECK
Goes to Camp!

HEIDI HECKELBECK
Is a Flower Girl

HEIDI HECKELBECK
Gets the Sniffles

By Wanda Coven

Illustrated by Priscilla Burris

LITTLE SIMON

New York   London   Toronto   Sydney   New Delhi

LITTLE SIMON
An imprint of Simon & Schuster Children's Publishing Division
1230 Avenue of the Americas, New York, New York 10020
This Little Simon bind-up edition September 2017
Heidi Heckelbeck Goes to Camp! copyright © 2013 by Simon & Schuster, Inc.
Heidi Heckelbeck Is a Flower Girl and *Heidi Heckelbeck Gets the Sniffles* copyright © 2014 by Simon & Schuster, Inc. All rights reserved, including the right of reproduction in whole or in part in any form. LITTLE SIMON is a registered trademark of Simon & Schuster, Inc., and associated colophon is a trademark of Simon & Schuster, Inc. For information about special discounts for bulk purchases, please contact Simon & Schuster Special Sales at 1-866-506-1949 or business@simonandschuster.com. The Simon & Schuster Speakers Bureau can bring authors to your live event. For more information or to book an event contact the Simon & Schuster Speakers Bureau at 1-866-248-3049 or visit our website at www.simonspeakers.com.
Manufactured in the United States of America 0817 MTN
10 9 8 7 6 5 4 3 2 1
Library of Congress Control Number 2017940661
ISBN 978-1-5344-0937-8
ISBN 978-1-4424-6482-7 (*Heidi Heckelbeck Goes to Camp!* eBook)
ISBN 978-1-4814-0500-3 (*Heidi Heckelbeck Is a Flower Girl* eBook)
ISBN 978-1-4814-1364-0 (*Heidi Heckelbeck Gets the Sniffles* eBook)
These titles were previously published individually in hardcover and paperback by Little Simon.

CONTENTS

CONTENTS

Chapter 1

A TRUNK FULL OF SPELLS

"Oogie da boinga!" Heidi Heckelbeck said as she grabbed a chocolate chip cookie from the dessert plate.

"What's that supposed to mean?" asked Henry.

"Lucy told me about it," Heidi said. "It means 'wahoo!' at Camp Dakota."

"It also means you have camp spirit," said Dad.

"Well, I have oogie da boinga too," said Henry. "So why can't I go to sleepaway camp?"

"Because you're a SHRIMP," Heidi said.

"Am not."

"Are too."

"Soon Henry will be old enough for sleepaway camp too," Mom said.

"It's going to feel like FOREVER until I'm old enough," said Henry.

"Trust me," Dad said. "It'll go fast."

"And so will this evening if we don't hop to it," said Mom.

"You two go and pack," said Dad. "Henry and I will do the dishes."

Heidi and her best friend, Lucy Lancaster, were leaving for Camp Dakota in the morning. Lucy had gone to Camp Dakota last summer. Now Heidi and Lucy would get to go together for two whole weeks!

Heidi's clothes lay in piles on her bed. Mom had ironed name tags on to all of Heidi's belongings.

"Let's check off the last few things," Mom said.

"Okay," said Heidi.

✓ Sneakers
✓ Flip-flops
✓ Binoculars
✓ Baseball cap
✓ Socks
✓ Stationery
✓ Goggles
✓ Raincoat
✓ Swimsuits
✓ Towels
✓ Pillow
✓ Bathroom kit
Tap shoes
Laundry bag

"Now all I need are my tap shoes and a laundry bag."

Heidi grabbed the shoe box from the shelf in her closet. She had tried tap in the school talent show, but that didn't count because she had used a tap-dancing spell. Now she wanted to learn for real.

Mom took one last look at the packing list. "I'll get you a laundry bag from the linen closet," she said.

As soon as Mom left the room, Heidi thought of something else she wanted to pack—something super-important. She kneeled on the carpet

and pulled her keepsake box out from under the bed. She opened the box and took out two things: her *Book of Spells* and her Witches of Westwick medallion. *Mom would never allow me to take these,* thought Heidi. *But what if there's an emergency?*

Heidi looked up and listened for her mom. Then she lifted a stack of clothes and carefully tucked her *Book of Spells* and medallion at the bottom of the trunk. She patted down her clothes as Mom walked back into the room.

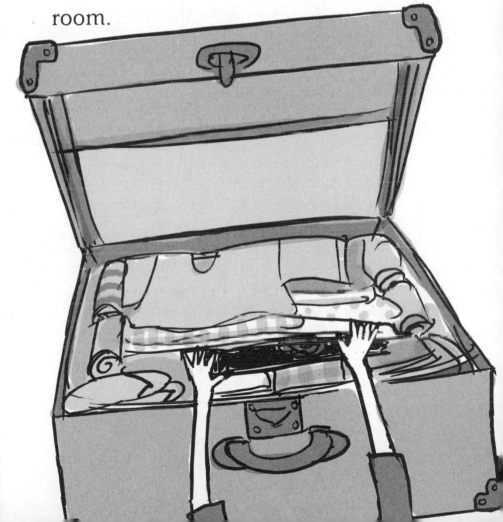

"That's it," said Mom, tossing a laundry bag to Heidi. "You're all packed for camp."

"Oogie da boinga!" said Heidi.

Then she shut and latched her trunk.

WHO'S SHE?

Heidi met Lucy at the Brewster Elementary parking lot. The bus for Camp Dakota had arrived. Some kids had already boarded.

"Time to go!" Heidi said.

She hugged her mom and dad good-bye.

Heidi turned to Henry. "You know what's weird?" she said. "I'm going to miss you."

"I'll miss you too," Henry said. "Write me, okay?"

"Promise," said Heidi. She high-fived her little brother.

Heidi slung her backpack over her shoulder and boarded the bus with Lucy. The girls waved as the bus pulled out. Then they looked at each other and squealed.

"This is going to be the BEST two weeks EVER!" Heidi said.

"I know," said Lucy. "And I can't

wait for you to meet my two camp friends, Jill and Bree."

"Me too," Heidi said.

During the ride the girls played hangman and drew pictures of ladybugs and unicorns. Soon the bus

pulled onto a dirt road lined with pine trees. Lucy pointed to the cabins and the lake at the end of the road. A bunch of campers greeted the bus in the parking lot.

"There they are!" shouted Lucy, waving at her friends from the bus window. She pointed them out to Heidi.

Heidi peeked at the girls. Jill had shoulder-length brown hair, brown eyes, and freckles. Bree had short blond hair and blue eyes. Both girls bounced up and down and waved. *Wow, they sure are happy to see Lucy,* she thought.

Heidi turned to say something to Lucy, but Lucy was already getting off the bus.

"Hey, wait for me!" shouted Heidi, bumping the seats with her backpack as she ran down the aisle.

But no one was listening to Heidi.

Jill, Bree, and Lucy clasped arms and danced in a circle. Then they took turns doing a secret handshake. Heidi tried to follow their moves. It started with a regular handshake, followed by a thumb clasp, a palm slide, and latched fingertips. They topped it off with fist taps, then peace signs across

their eyes. This made Heidi feel a bit left out. Luckily, Lucy noticed.

"This is my friend Heidi," said Lucy.

Jill and Bree stopped talking and looked Heidi up and down.

"Oh, hi," they both said. Then they each grabbed Lucy by an arm.

"Come on, Lucy," said Jill. "Want to see our cabin?" They took off skipping down the path.

Heidi walked behind the girls and listened to them talk. They went on and on about all the fun things they had done last summer.

Some camp greeters followed with Lucy's and Heidi's trunks.

"Remember that huge rainstorm and the big mudslide we made on Huckleberry Hill?" asked Bree.

"That was SO fun," Lucy said.

"I didn't even notice when I scraped my arm!" said Jill.

"I didn't think we'd ever get all that

mud off! It was really caked on!" said Bree.

"What about the time we snuck cookies from the dining room?" asked Lucy.

"We almost got caught," Jill said.

"That was the best part!" said Lucy.

"How about the HAUNTED COMB that flew across the cabin in the middle of the night?" Bree said.

"You threw it and you know it!" said Lucy.

"Did not!" said Bree. "That comb really WAS haunted. Last year was the best!"

The girls kept talking and giggling as they walked up the log stairs to cabin eight. The cabin had a view of the lake. Heidi heard the hum of a motorboat in the distance. The sun sparkled on the water. *I've only been at camp for ten minutes,* she thought. *But instead of feeling excited, I feel all alone.*

CLOSETS AND QUILTS

"Lucy, this bed is yours," Bree said as she pointed to a blue-and-white-striped mattress on a metal cot.

Lucy's bed was in between Jill's and Bree's.

Lucy plopped her backpack on the bed. "Where's Heidi going to sleep?"

"Over there, I guess," said Jill as she pointed to a bed on the other side of the cabin. The only other bed on that side was the counselor's.

"Is that okay with you, Heidi?" Lucy asked.

Heidi looked at the lonely bed in

the corner. *No!* she thought. *It's not okay! Why can't Lucy sleep on MY side of the cabin and Jill and Bree sleep on the OTHER side? That would be fair.* But Heidi didn't dare complain. She didn't want Lucy's friends to think she was a baby.

"Sure, it's fine," said Heidi.

She walked over and sat on her mattress. She looked around the cabin. Everyone had a bed and an orange crate. Jill and Bree had already

filled their crates with their bathroom kits, flashlights, bug spray, batteries, and stationery. The back of the cabin had five changing closets. Each one had a cotton curtain with a different print.

There were checks, stripes, flowers, and polka dots. One curtain was plain.

The camp greeters set Lucy's and Heidi's trunks beside their beds and left.

"Let's make your bed, Lucy!" said Bree.

Jill and Bree had already made their beds. Jill's had a swirly polka-dot quilt, and Bree's had a pink-and-orange daisy quilt.

"What does your quilt look like, Lucy?" asked Bree.

"Mine has butterflies," Lucy said as she pulled her quilt from her trunk.

"It's SO cute!" said Jill.

"How about you, Heidi?" asked Lucy. "What's your quilt like?"

"Mine's boring purple with a whole bunch of nothing," said Heidi.

"Oh, I LOVE purple!" Lucy said, trying to make it sound wonderful.

Jill and Bree didn't say anything.

Then the girls picked out closets.

"The
one with
the pink-checked
curtain is yours,"
Bree said.

"Okay," said Lucy. "Heidi,
you can have the one on the other
side of mine."

Heidi looked at her closet. It had a
plain blue curtain that was lopsided.
One of the thumbtacks had fallen out.

Heidi hung up her stuff. Then a
loud bell rang.

"Lunchtime!" said Jill.

Heidi followed the girls out the door. She didn't feel hungry, but she did feel something. It was the same feeling she'd had when she was the new girl at school. She felt like an alien.

Chapter 4

RAH, RAH

Voices chattered and silverware rattled in the log-cabin dining hall. The girls stopped next to the door to look at their table assignments.

"We're at table four," Lucy said, pointing to a list of names.

The girls piled into the dining hall,

but the door snapped shut in Heidi's face. Lucy turned back and opened the door.

"Come on, Heidi," she said.

Heidi followed the girls to table four. Lucy sat next to Jill and Bree. Heidi found an empty seat next to the counselor at the head of the table.

Everyone chatted except Heidi. She just stared at the bowls of food on the table: taco shells, ground beef, corn bread, lettuce, and tomatoes. She helped herself to a glass of red punch.

Even aliens get thirsty, she thought.

Then the counselor tapped her glass with a butter knife. All the girls at the table stopped talking.

"As most of you know, I'm Lila, cabin eight's counselor," she said. "Welcome to Camp Dakota!"

Lila had long, straight brown hair and friendly blue eyes. She looked like an athlete, and she had a golden sun tan.

Lila looked around the table and then turned to Heidi. "You must be Heidi."

"I'm glad to have you in my cabin. Tell me, is there anything special you'd like to do at camp?"

"I'd like to tap-dance," said Heidi.

"I like tap too," said Lila. "Did you know I'm the dance teacher?"

Heidi shook her head.

"Well, I am," Lila said. "We're going to have a blast."

Heidi smiled. *Lila's nice,* she thought. *Maybe camp won't be so bad after all.* She ate half a taco and had some more punch.

At the end of lunch, Lila walked to the front of the dining hall. Two other counselors ran to join her—one had red hair in a ponytail and the other had short black hair.

"Welcome to Camp Dakota!" the red-haired girl said. "I'm Jenna."

"I'm Paige," said the black-haired girl.

"I'm Lila."

"First, we have to go over camp rules," said Paige. "So listen up! Rule number one: Always have a buddy at the beach."

Lila held up a big sign that said BUDDY UP!

"Rule number two: Always stay on the camp's grounds," Jenna said.

Paige held up a sign that had a map of the camp. It said STAY PUT!

"Rule number three: Always follow the counselors' instructions," said Lila.

Jenna held up a sign that said WHO'S THE BOSS? Then she flipped it over, and it said WE ARE!

"Now for the camp no-no's," said Jenna.

"No matches."

"No hair-dryers."

"No hand-held devices."

"No water balloons or shaving cream!"

"Unless we say so!" added Lila.

"No radios," continued Jenna.

"No food in the cabins."

"No rubber duckies!"

"And no rubber chickens!"

The campers laughed.

"Okay, we're only joking about the rubber duckies and chickens," Paige

said. "But we're not kidding when we say 'No monkey business.' Follow the rules and be safe."

"Okay, sign-up sheets for activities are at the back of the room!" said Lila. "If you have any questions, come see us."

Everyone began to talk and clear dishes. Heidi scraped the food from her plate into the trash and put her dishes into a plastic tub. Then she headed for the sign-up tables. Jill and Bree were still stuck to Lucy like Super

Glue. Heidi stood behind them.

"What are you going to sign up for?" asked Lucy.

"Tap-dance, riding, arts and crafts, swimming, and basketball," Heidi said excitedly.

"Me too!" squealed Lucy. "Except

instead of tap, I'm going to take gymnastics with Jill and Bree."

"Sounds good," said Heidi. *Except for the part about Jill and Bree,* she thought.

"So, what do you think of camp so far?" asked Lucy. "Isn't it fun?"

"It's a blast," Heidi said. "Rah, rah."

KER-FLUNK!

Heidi stuffed her tap shoes in her backpack.

"See you at riding!" Lucy said as she left for gymnastics.

Jill and Bree followed Lucy down the cabin stairs. They didn't say good-bye to Heidi.

I wonder why those two don't like me, Heidi wondered. She slung her backpack over her shoulder and headed for tap class.

Lila taught the class how to shuffle.

"I want you to brush the floor with the ball of your foot forward and backward," she said. "Like this."

Lila brushed her foot across the

floor from front to back. "Try it with me," said Lila.

Heidi did a shuffle. She liked it when her tap shoes clacked on the floor. Then Lila taught the class to shim sham.

"A shim sham is a shuffle and a step," said Lila as she turned on some music.

The class did a combination of steps: Shim sham. Jump. Toe. Step. They did it again and again to the music. *This is so much fun!* thought Heidi. *I can't wait to show Lucy.* Then Heidi's heart sank. She remembered that Lucy had been taken over by Jill and Bree. *Maybe they'll be nicer to me at riding,* she thought.

Heidi arrived at the riding ring in a sweatshirt, jeans, and scuffed cowboy boots. She'd had to borrow a stinky helmet from the stable. Lucy, Jill, and

Bree had on riding pants, hunting coats, and fancy riding helmets. Bree stared at Heidi's outfit.

"Are you really going to ride in THAT?" asked Bree.

Heidi looked down at her outfit.

"We all wore jeans when we rode last year," Lucy said. "Remember?"

"Let's just go and choose our horses," said Jill.

The girls ran to the stables. Each stall had a name above the door. Lucy chose a horse named Peaches. Jill chose Tinkerbell, and Bree chose Sundance. Heidi got a horse named Fred.

"He's gentle," said Jenna. "And he always follows the other horses."

Jenna helped Heidi get into her saddle. But Fred did not follow the other horses. He stood still, eating grass. Jenna tried to get Fred to move. But Fred wouldn't budge.

Heidi sighed. *Not even a dumb horse likes me,* she thought.

Later, in swim class, everyone had to pick a buddy.

"Want to be buddies?" asked Lucy.

"Sure," Heidi said.

First the girls had to take a swim test. Heidi had never gone swimming in a lake before. The lake water looked dark and murky. *What if there are snapping turtles in there?* Heidi

thought. She tightly shut her eyes and jumped in the water.

Heidi then swam a few strokes, but all she could think about were snapping turtles. She was so scared that she grabbed the safety pole before the test was over. That meant Heidi had flunked the test. Now she would be placed in Beginners.

In the meantime, Lucy, Bree, and Jill had passed

the test with flying colors, so they were placed in Intermediates.

All day everything seemed to go wrong. On the basketball court nobody passed the ball to Heidi. In

arts and crafts, they ran out of beads, so Heidi had to braid the strings of her friendship bracelets instead. At Campfire, Heidi got squished between two strange girls. And to top it off, the smoke blew right into her face.

I'm getting out of here, thought Heidi.

She wiggled off the log and ran back to the cabin.

Nobody noticed
Heidi had gone.

Chapter 6

SUGAR AND SPICE

Heidi sat on her bed and pulled out a
sheet of turtle stationery. She wrote:

Dear Henry,

Camp stinks. The beds
are really squeaky. The
bathrooms are smelly. And
the lake is full of snapping

turtles. The only friends I have are mosquitoes.

Yours truly,

Heidi

PS Stay out of my room—or else!

Heidi stuck the letter in an envelope and sighed. *Jill and Bree have taken my best friend prisoner,* she thought. *If only they liked me, then camp would be fun.* Suddenly, Heidi had a wild idea. *What if I MAKE them like me?*

Heidi flung open her trunk and pulled out her *Book of Spells*. She flipped through the pages and found a spell called A Friendly Foe. *Perfect,* she thought. *A friendly foe is an enemy who becomes a friend.* She read over the spell.

A Friendly Foe

Do people dislike you for no reason? Are you the kind of witch who always feels left out? Would you like to make friends with your enemies? Then this is the spell for you!

Ingredients:
1 cup of fruit punch
1 stick of powdered candy
1 teaspoon of cinnamon sugar
1 friendship bracelet for each foe
1 empty water bottle

Shake all the ingredients together in the water bottle. Hold your Witches of Westwick medallion in your left hand. Close your eyes and place your right hand over the bottle.

Chant the following words:

Oh, SWEET MAGICAL BREW
FILLED WITH SUGAR AND SPICE,
MAKE [NAME OF PERSON(S)]
GO FROM MEAN TO NICE!

Remove the bracelets.
When the bracelets are dry,
the spell has been cast.

Note: If the bracelet has contact with water, the spell will wear off.

Heidi skipped over the note in small letters at the bottom of the spell and read back over the list of ingredients. Then she grabbed an empty sports water bottle from her orange crate. *I can get the fruit punch and cinnamon sugar from the dining hall,* she thought. *The camp store sells powdered candy. And I can use the friendship bracelets I made in arts and crafts. So simple!*

Heidi memorized the spell. Then she hid her *Book of Spells* at the bottom of her trunk. She heard campers talking as they walked back to their cabins. *Campfire must be over,* she thought. She quickly put on her panda pajamas and slipped into bed.

Tomorrow is going to be a better day. . . .

SHA-ZiNG!

The next day Jill, Bree, and Lucy left for breakfast without Heidi.

"Hurry up!" called Lucy from the stairs.

"Be right there," Heidi called back.

Heidi dumped her earplugs onto the bed. *I'll hide the cinnamon sugar in my earplug case,* she thought. She shoved the empty case into her pocket, grabbed the water bottle, and ran to the dining hall.

At breakfast Heidi slipped a teaspoon into her pocket. Then she filled her water bottle with one cup of fruit punch. Bree gave her a funny look. Heidi smiled and excused herself from the table. She found the cinnamon sugar at the toaster station. She poured some sugar into her earplug case and snapped the lid shut.

"What are you up to?" asked Lucy.

Heidi jumped. "Oh, nothing."

"Hmm," said Lucy. "Well, we should get going. The first activity is about to start."

The girls left the dining hall and headed toward their activities.

Heidi had some free time after tap. She raced to the camp store and bought two striped straws filled with powdered candy. *I'll use cherry for the spell,* she thought. *And I'll keep the grape one for me.* Then she zoomed back to the empty cabin. Heidi had to

hurry. The girls would be back soon to change before riding.

Heidi tore the top off the cherry straw and dumped the red powder into the fruit punch. Then she added a teaspoon of cinnamon sugar. Heidi shook the water bottle. Then she opened it back up and dropped two friendship bracelets inside. She held

her medallion in one
of her hands. Then
she shut her eyes,
placed her other
hand over the
bottle, and
chanted
the spell.
The mixture
bubbled for a few moments. Then it
became still.

Heidi took the friendship bracelets
out of the bottle with her finger. In a
few moments they were dry . . . and
magical!

When Jill and Bree returned to change, Heidi handed the bewitched bracelets to them.

"Uh, thanks?" Bree said, not really sure what to say.

Heidi gave a regular bracelet to Lucy.

The girls slipped on their bracelets.

Sha-zing!

The magic began to work.

"Wow," said Bree. "This is the most beautiful friendship bracelet I've ever seen!"

"Same with mine," Jill said.

Jill and Bree each hooked an elbow with

Heidi and walked with her to the stables. Lucy hurried after them.

At the stables Jill gave the best horse to Heidi. "I want you to ride Tinkerbell today," she said. "She's the nicest horse of all."

"Thanks!" said Heidi.

All afternoon Jill and Bree did everything to please Heidi.

"Sit with me!" begged Jill.

"Be my partner!" pleaded Bree.

"You are the BEST artist, Heidi!"

"Please show us your tap steps!"

"Be my best friend!"

"No, be MINE!"

On the dock at swimming, Lucy pulled Heidi aside. "What on earth is going on?" she asked.

"Beats me," Heidi said, trying not to smile. "But it's a nice change—don't you think?"

"It's a little weird, if you ask me," said Lucy.

Then Heidi, Jill, and Bree held hands and jumped off the float.

Splash!

But when they popped up for air, something had changed.

"What are YOU doing here?" asked Bree.

"Aren't you in Beginners?" added Jill.

Oh no! Heidi thought. *The spell has worn off!* She swam to the ladder. Then

Heidi wrapped herself in a towel, slipped on her flip-flops, and hurried to the cabin. *If only they had liked me for real,* she thought. *But it was just the dumb spell.* Heidi kicked a pinecone on the path.

NOW what am I going to do?

Chapter 8

CHICKEN TALK

"You're back early," Lila said as Heidi walked into the cabin.

Heidi tried to say something, but she couldn't. Her eyes filled with tears.

"Come sit," said Lila. She spread a towel across her bed and offered Heidi a big box of pink tissues.

Heidi sat down and pulled out a tissue.

"What's up?" asked Lila.

"It's Jill and Bree," Heidi said in between sniffles. "They're mean to me, and they hog all of Lucy's time."

"Have you talked to them about it?" asked Lila.

"No," said Heidi.

"Well, you should," said Lila. "You need to find out what's going on."

"I'm too chicken," said Heidi. "What if they really hate me?"

Lila patted Heidi on the back. "They have no reason to hate you," she said. "They're probably just jealous."

"JEALOUS?" questioned Heidi. "Of ME?"

"Yes, of *you*," said Lila. "You're a total package!"

Heidi wiped her nose with a tissue. "Package of WHAT?" she asked.

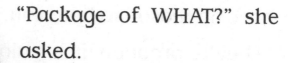

Lila smiled at Heidi. "Package of F-U-N," she said, messing up Heidi's wet hair.

Heidi let out a small laugh.

"Listen, I have to get ready for my next class," said Lila, getting up. "Tell me how it goes."

"*B-r-r-r-ock, b-r-r-r-ock,*" squawked Heidi.

"You can't chicken out," said Lila. "Be brave!"

Lila gave Heidi a hug. "Your bathing suit got me all wet," she said.

"That's because I'm a wet chicken," said Heidi.

"You need to be a *brave* chicken," said Lila. Then she hurried down the steps.

Heidi got dressed in her changing closet. Then she flopped onto her bed and waited for the girls to come back from swimming. *What am I going to say?* she thought. *Hey, guys. Why do you hate me so much?*

Chapter 9

OOGiE DA BOiNGA!

The cabin door banged open. Heidi jumped to her feet.

"What's up, Heidi?" asked Lucy. "Everything okay?"

"Not really," said Heidi.

"What's wrong?" asked Lucy.

Heidi looked at Jill and Bree. She

pushed the chicken thoughts out of her head. "How come you guys are so mean to me?" she asked. "I really don't like to be treated that way."

Jill and Bree looked surprised, but neither one said a word.

"Heidi's right, you know," said Lucy. "You haven't been nice to her at all. How come?"

Jill and Bree looked at each other. Then Jill put up her hands. "Okay, okay," she said. "I guess we were afraid that Heidi had taken our place. We didn't want to lose Lucy as our friend."

"Are you kidding?" asked Lucy. "You're not going to lose me as a friend. I'll always be friends with you!" Then she turned to Heidi. "And I'll always be friends with Heidi, too."

Lucy smiled at Heidi.

"Why can't we *all* be friends?"

asked Heidi. "I'm really not an evil, friend-stealing monster, you know."

"Now THAT would be an ugly monster," Bree said, cracking a smile.

The girls all laughed.

"I guess we HAVE been kind of rotten," admitted Jill.

"I'm sorry that we made you feel bad, Heidi," said Bree.

Heidi felt so relieved. "I only wish I had said something sooner," she replied.

"I wish I had too," said Lucy. She put her hand in front of Heidi. "Friends?" she asked.

Heidi put her hand on top of Lucy's. "Friends," she said.

Jill and Bree put their hands on top of the others. "Friends," they said.

"You know what?" Heidi said. "I just
felt it for the first time at camp!"

"What?" asked Lucy.

"Oogie da boinga!" said Heidi.

Lucy's eyes got wide. "I felt it too!" she said. "Oogie da boinga!"

"So did I!" said Jill.

"Me too!" said Bree.

"Oogie da boinga!" they all said together.

Lucy, Jill, and Bree changed out of their wet swimsuits. Then all four girls walked arm in arm to lunch.

Chapter 10

"DAKOTA" MEANS "FRiENDS"

A week later Heidi sat on her bed and wrote another letter to her brother.

Dear Henry,

You know what stinks most about camp? It's almost over. I come home in three days! Lucy and I are going to miss our cabinmates and counselor so much. I love my friends. Did

you know "Dakota" is a Native
American word for "friends"?
Pretty cool.

Last night we had a shaving
cream fight. Everyone got a can
of shaving cream. Then we had
a FOAM WAR. Here's a picture of
us with foam hairdos and foam
beards. Like Lucy's mohawk?

Big news! I can ride a horse! My horse, Fred, didn't like me at first. He could tell I was a scaredy-cat, but now we're buds. I sneak him carrots and sugar cubes from the dining hall every day.

One of my favorite things about camp is Campfire. The

counselors play
guitars, and we sing
songs and roast
marshmallows. I ate
five s'mores last
night!

Guess what? We won the
neatest cabin award! We got
FREE candy at the camp store.
I picked fireballs, root beer
barrels, and a Tootsie Pop.

Tonight we're going to write our names on the cabin wall. We found names of campers from the 1920s! I wonder what camp was like in those days? Did they have shaving cream fights? Did they even HAVE shaving cream back then?

Tomorrow night is the talent show. I'm doing a tap routine (without spells).

See ya soon, shrimp!

Love,

Heidi

PS I didn't see a single snapping turtle!

PPS I can't wait for BOTH of us to come back next time.

PPPS Oogie da boinga!

CONTENTS

Chapter 1

MiSS HARRiET'S

Heidi Heckelbeck had a lot on her mind. She had been spying on Principal Pennypacker for more than a week because she was pretty sure he was a witch. Why else would he have a *Book of Spells* in his office? At least, that's what the book looked like. Now she just had to prove he was a witch. And on top of her witch detective work, Heidi had also been asked to be a flower girl in her aunt Sophie's wedding.

Aunt Sophie was Dad's sister, and soon she was going to marry Uncle Ned in the Heckelbecks' backyard.

Well, Uncle Ned wasn't actually Heidi's uncle *yet*—not until after the wedding—but Heidi and Henry had called him Uncle Ned ever since he'd gotten engaged to Aunt Sophie. Now Heidi had to go dress shopping.

Ugh, thought Heidi as she stood in the middle of Miss Harriet's dress

shop. She had never shopped for a fancy dress before. Now she was surrounded by them. Miss Harriet looked Heidi up and down. Then she sifted through the dress racks and pulled out dresses in a rainbow of pastel colors: strawberry, mint, yellow, cream, and blue.

"You'll make an enchanting flower girl in any one of these," she said, holding the flouncy dresses in front of Heidi.

Heidi frowned. *I'll look like a poofy powder puff in any one of those dresses,* she thought. It wasn't that Heidi hated dresses. It's just that they weren't exactly her style. She was more of an everyday girl.

Heidi followed her mother into the dressing room.

Then she pulled off her favorite kitty cat top and jean skirt. Heidi left on her black-and-white-striped tights and sneakers. Then she slipped a strawberry dress over her head. Mom tied the satin sash around Heidi's waist. The dress had a scratchy skirt that stuck out like a giant lampshade.

"I feel like I'm caught in a big fishing net," complained Heidi. "And the skirt part is itchy."

"It's called crinoline," said Heidi's mom. "It's a very fancy dress material."

Heidi glanced in the mirror. "It looks like something Smell-a-nie would wear," she said.

Melanie Maplethorpe, also known as Smell-a-nie, was Heidi's worst enemy.

"Forget Melanie," said Mom. "That

dress is too pink with your red hair. Let's try another one."

Heidi tried on another dress, and another and another.

The mint dress made her look like she hadn't slept in a week. The yellow dress made her look like a glass of lemonade. And the cream dress made her look like a miniature bride. Then Mom zipped the blue dress and tied the sash.

Heidi looked in the mirror. She turned this way and that while she looked at herself.

"I love it," said Mom.

"'Love' is such a strong word," said Heidi.

"But it looks very good on you," said Mom.

Heidi scratched her neck. "The ruffles make me itch," she said.

"You will get used to them," said Mom. "You won't even realize they're there when you walk down the aisle."

"Merg," said Heidi.

"Beautiful," said Mom.

"Perfect!" exclaimed Miss Harriet.

"Except for the black-and-white-striped tights and sneakers."

Miss Harriet scurried into another room and came back with a pair of light blue ballet flats. She also brought Heidi a basket to hold her flower petals. Heidi had been told a flower girl had to sprinkle flower petals all along the wedding aisle.

Heidi slipped on the blue flats and stared at her feet. *Eww,* she thought as she wrinkled her nose.

Click! Miss Harriet snapped Heidi's picture.

"Perfect!" said Miss Harriet as she hurried to her computer to download the picture. "I'll give you a copy to take home."

The flash had made Heidi see spots. She rubbed her eyes. Then she stared at herself again in the mirror.

"Can I at least wear my blue-and-white-striped tights with this girly outfit?" asked Heidi.

"Sure," Mom said. "Be your own flower girl!"

And that made Heidi feel a teeny bit better.

Chapter 2

A BAD DREAM

Henry held a small sofa pillow in his hands like a tea tray. On top of the pillow sat a red ring pop. He walked slowly across the kitchen, being careful not to drop the ring pop.

"Look at me!" he cried. "I'm a RING BEAR!"

Heidi rolled her eyes.

"You mean a ring bear-ER," she said.

"Whatever," said Henry. He circled the kitchen table. "I get to carry the rings that Uncle Ned and Aunt Sophie give each other."

"Big whoop," said Heidi.

"I also get to wear a tuxedo," Henry added.

"Double big whoop," said Heidi.

"Your aunt Sophie's wedding *is* a very big whoop," Dad said.

"All I know is that I have to wear a froofy party dress," said Heidi.

"I can't wait to see THAT," said Henry.

"Merg," growled Heidi as she stomped out of the room.

That night Heidi had a bad dream about the wedding. In her dream, the skirt on her fancy party dress had grown enormous. The ruffles around her neck had climbed all the way up to her chin. Then she realized it was her turn to walk down the aisle. The guests all stared at her. Heidi tried

to bend over to pick up her basket of petals, but she couldn't. She tried again and tipped over. Heidi lay on her stomach, kicking her feet, like a bug in a swimming pool.

Then, *bing!* Just like that, she woke up, except she was still kicking. Heidi had gotten all twisted in her covers. Finally she wriggled free of the sheets and sighed in relief.

Later at school, Heidi told her friend Lucy Lancaster about the wedding and the flower girl dress.

"You're so lucky!" Lucy exclaimed. "I've always wanted to be in a wedding."

"Do you want to trade places?" asked Heidi.

"Very funny," said Lucy. "So, what's your dress look like?"

"I brought a picture," Heidi said. "But you have to promise not to laugh."

"Promise," said Lucy.

Heidi reached into her back pocket and pulled out the photo Miss Harriet

had taken in the store. She started to hand it to Lucy, but before Lucy got it, Melanie snatched it out of Heidi's hand.

"Let ME see!" cried Melanie.

"Hey, that's MINE!" cried Heidi.

Melanie looked at the picture and squealed with laughter.

"Oh my gosh," cried Smell-a-nie in between giggles. "That dress is SO icky!"

Stanley Stonewrecker snuck up behind Melanie and grabbed the photo out of her hand. Melanie kept right on laughing as Stanley looked at the picture.

"Wow, Heidi," said Stanley as he handed the picture back to Heidi. "You look great in that dress."

Melanie huffed in disgust.

Lucy peeked at the photo. "Stanley's right, you do look great," she said. "And PS, Melanie, if you think THAT dress is icky, you should get a whole new wardrobe."

Melanie folded her arms and turned up her nose.

"I'll bet Heidi won't even be able to walk in that dress," said Melanie. "She'll probably trip and fall when she walks down the aisle."

Heidi couldn't believe what Melanie had just said. It was as if she knew Heidi had had a bad dream about falling down at the wedding. *How does she do that?* Heidi thought. *And what if I really do fall down in front of everybody?*

It was too awful to think about.

Chapter 3

LiLAC POWDER

On Saturday, Heidi helped Aunt Trudy clean out her basement. Aunt Trudy was Mom's sister, and she was also a witch. Aunt Trudy had the best castoffs. Heidi had gotten things like glass beads, jeweled charms, funky buttons, pressed flowers, and empty makeup containers. Cleaning at her aunt's house was like going on a treasure hunt.

Today, Aunt Trudy had a whole list of things for Heidi to do. She had her fold clothes for giveaway boxes, pack books for the library book drive, and clean shelves. On one shelf Heidi found a shoe box filled with seashells, sea glass, and dried starfish. She poked through the box.

"These shells are so pretty," Heidi said.

Aunt Trudy looked over her shoulder. "I collected them ages ago," she said. "Feel free to take them, or I'll put them in a giveaway box."

Heidi set the shoe box in her take-home pile. Then she got back to work. Heidi thought about the wedding as she dusted off a shelf.

"Aunt Trudy, have you ever been a flower girl?" she asked.

Aunt Trudy tossed a book into one of the boxes. "No," she said. "But I always dreamed of being one."

"You did?" questioned Heidi. "Why?"

"Because being a flower girl is a special honor," said Aunt Trudy. "And you also get to wear a fancy dress and walk down the aisle."

"Yuck," said Heidi. "That's the worst part, if you ask me."

"Don't you like to dress up?" asked Aunt Trudy.

"Well, sometimes," admitted Heidi. "I just don't like to be in the spotlight."

"Why not?" said Aunt Trudy.

"Because what if I trip and fall in front of all the guests?"

Aunt Trudy looked over the top of her glasses. "So what if you did?" she said. "It would make a good story."

"I just don't like it," said Heidi.

Aunt Trudy put her arm around her niece. "Being in the spotlight is special," she said. "And your aunt Sophie picked you to be her flower girl because she loves you and thinks you'll do a good job."

"I know," mumbled Heidi.

"Just pretend you're on a fashion show runway in Paris," Aunt Trudy said.

Heidi tried to picture herself on a runway in Paris. It actually sounded kind of fun.

Then her aunt picked up a pile of old winter clothes and put them on a card table in front of Heidi.

"Let's fold these and put them in a shopping bag," Aunt Trudy said.

Heidi nodded and pulled a sweater

from the pile. Something fell onto the floor. It was a little satchel. *It must've been wrapped in the sweater,* thought Heidi. She picked up the satchel and undid the drawstring. The bag was filled with purple powder. Heidi sniffed the powder. *Ah-choo! Ah-choo! Ah-choo!*

"Bless you!" said Aunt Trudy. She gave Heidi a tissue, and then she began to laugh.

"What's so funny?" Heidi asked, wiping her nose.

"The lilac powder!" said Aunt Trudy. "Lilac powder makes witches sneeze."

"It does?"

"Yup, every time," Aunt Trudy said.

Heidi found this *very* interesting.

"Does it work on ALL witches?" she asked.

"Every last one."

Wow, Heidi thought. *I could use this lilac powder on Principal Pennypacker. If he sneezes, I'll know for sure he's a witch.*

"May I take this

satchel home?" Heidi asked.

"Sure," said Aunt Trudy as she began to sweep the floor. "I've got plenty of lilac powder."

Heidi stuffed the satchel into her pocket. She had forgotten all about being a flower girl. Now all she could think about was how to get Principal Pennypacker to smell the lilac powder.

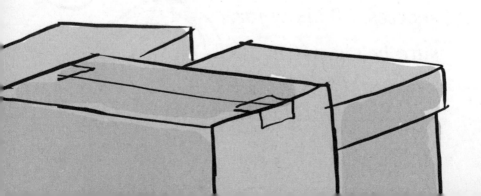

Chapter 4

FLOWER POWER

On Monday, Heidi spied on Principal Pennypacker at school. She hadn't figured out exactly how she was going to get him to sniff the powder, but she had to find a way. She sat on the school steps and watched the principal oversee the children at

drop-off. He waved and talked to the parents who had rolled down their car windows. *Hmm,* thought Heidi. *Drop-off is too busy. I'll have to find a better time.*

On the way to art class Heidi saw

Principal Pennypacker giving a tour
to a mother and two children. Heidi
remembered what it was like to be
new. *I'm sure glad that's not me,* she
thought.

Heidi paused at the water fountain,

and as she drank she kept an eye on the principal. He showed the family the student artwork hanging in the hallway. *I'll never get him to sniff the lilac powder when he's on a school tour,* she thought. Heidi wiped her mouth with the back of her hand and continued down the hall. Principal Pennypacker smiled as she passed by.

At lunch Heidi chose a seat near the faculty table. The principal sat at the head of the table. She watched him eat a slice of pizza. *If only I could sprinkle a little lilac powder on his pizza,* thought Heidi. But it would be way too obvious.

Lucy and Bruce Bickerson set their lunch trays down next to Heidi.

"So, how's the whole flower girl thing going?" asked Lucy.

"Same," said Heidi. "Mostly boring and pretty dumb."

Lucy laughed. "You're so funny," she said. "Most girls would give anything to be a flower girl."

Heidi shrugged and pulled the cheese off her pizza.

"Not me," she said.

At recess Heidi stood in line for foursquare and watched Principal Pennypacker. He was talking to her teacher, Mrs. Welli. *Darn,* thought Heidi. *He's always with somebody.* Then she

noticed a patch of dandelions on the playing field behind the principal and her teacher. This gave Heidi an idea.

She stepped out of line, ran to the field, and began to pick dandelions. Then she pulled the satchel of lilac powder from  her pocket. Heidi undid the string and sprinkled the powder on the top of the flowers. Then she skipped toward the

principal with her bouquet.

"Hello, Heidi," said the principal. "I hear you're going to be in a wedding this weekend. What fun!"

"Sort of," Heidi said. Then she

held the flowers out in sniffing range. "Would you like to smell my fresh-picked flowers?"

Principal Pennypacker leaned over. "Why, I'd love to," he said.

He smelled the dandelions. Heidi waited for a big sneeze. But nothing

happened. She pulled the dandelions out from under the principal's nose and walked away. *That's weird,* she thought. Heidi sniffed the dandelions to see if the powder still worked.

Ah-choo! Ah-choo! Ah-choo!

Merg, thought Heidi as she tossed the dandelions into the bushes. *I guess Principal Pennypacker's not a witch after all.* She was a bit disappointed. It had been fun spying on him. *Oh well,* she thought, and ran back to the foursquare game.

Chapter 5

PiRATE BOOTY

Wedding talk was the only talk at the Heckelbeck house all week. On Friday a large van delivered tables, chairs, and a large white tent. On Saturday several people in matching aprons set the tables and cooked food in the Heckelbecks' kitchen. The wedding would begin at four o'clock that afternoon.

Soon it was time to get ready. Dad, Uncle Ned, and Henry got dressed in Henry's room. Heidi, Mom, Aunt Sophie, and Aunt Trudy got ready in Heidi's parents' bedroom. Mom clasped Aunt Sophie's pearl necklace. Aunt Trudy tied Heidi's sash and clipped a powder-blue flower in Heidi's hair.

"Hold still, missy!" said Aunt Trudy.

"But this dress is itching me!" said Heidi.

Heidi did her best to hold still. Then Henry burst into the bedroom in his tuxedo. He had a plastic sword in his hand and a black eye patch over his left eye.

"Ahoy, me hearties!" cried Henry as he jumped onto an ottoman and pretended to scan the horizon.

Heidi ignored Henry's behavior, but she studied his outfit.

"You look like a miniature man," she said.

Henry planted his fists on his hips. "Methinks I am a well-dressed pirate!" he said. "And my treasure chest is chock-full of loot."

"What kind of loot?" asked Heidi. "It better not be anything from my room."

"Sparkling jewels and dazzling gems!" shouted Henry. "And today I added a very valuable ring to my treasure."

Heidi had a funny feeling. She knew what kind of ring Henry had added to his loot. She ran across the room, grabbed Henry by the arm, and dragged him into the hall.

"Do you have Aunt Sophie's wedding ring?" asked Heidi.

"Of course!" said Henry. "I'm the RING BEAR!"

"The ring bear-ER," Heidi corrected. "Now, where is it?"

"What?" asked Henry.

"The RING!"

"It's in my treasure chest!" Henry said.

"Does Uncle Ned know you have it?"

"No," Henry admitted.

"Well, you better give it back," said Heidi.

"But Dad gave it to me!" argued Henry.

"I don't care if Dad gave it to you.

Get it NOW," said Heidi. "If Uncle Ned doesn't have the ring, he and Aunt Sophie won't be able to get married."

"Oh no!" said Henry. "Will you help me look for it?"

Heidi let out a heavy sigh. "Come on," she said. "We haven't got much time before the wedding begins."

Chapter 6

WHAT IF?

Henry flipped open the skull latch on his wooden pirate chest and emptied the contents onto the playroom floor. Heidi and Henry combed through the silver and gold plastic coins and beaded necklaces. Heidi spied a fake ring and a plastic hotdog in the pile, but there wasn't a wedding ring.

"I can't believe you really lost the ring," Heidi said.

"I didn't mean to," said Henry.

"Maybe it's in the toy chest," suggested Heidi.

She ran to the toy chest and flung open the lid. Then she began to toss puppets, dodge balls, and plastic army men over her shoulder. Henry found a kaleidoscope. He peeked in the lens and twisted the end of it.

Heidi glared at Henry. "Put that down!" she shouted. "Don't you know that you're in HUGE trouble?"

Henry dropped the kaleidoscope and began searching through the trunk. But there was no ring.

Heidi tipped over a tub full of sports equipment. Super Balls and tennis balls rolled across the floor.

"What if we don't find the ring?" asked Henry.

"Then there really won't be a wedding," said Heidi.

"And if there isn't a wedding, then what?"

"Then I won't have to wear this dumb dress," said Heidi.

"Hey, that's mean," Henry said.

"Besides, you look kind of pretty in that dress."

Heidi stopped searching and looked at her brother. "Thanks, little man," she said.

Then they carefully sorted through the sports equipment on the floor, but they still didn't find the ring.

They looked upstairs, downstairs, and under all the sofas and chairs. But the wedding ring was nowhere to be found.

"Let's face it," said Henry. "I'm dead."

"Pretty much," Heidi said. "But I have an idea."

RAZZLE-DAZZLE

"What's your idea?" asked Henry hopefully.

"Follow me," Heidi said.

They zoomed down the hall to Heidi's room.

"Shut the door," said Heidi.

Henry closed the door behind

them. Then Heidi knelt on the floor and pulled her *Book of Spells* and her Witches of Westwick medallion from under the bed.

"It's a good thing I'm a witch," said Heidi.

"You're not kidding," said Henry.

Heidi ran her finger down the Contents page and found the chapter called "Jewelry." She flipped through the pages to a spell called "Ring Replacer."

"What does it say?" Henry asked.

Heidi read the spell out loud.

*Has your favorite ring
fallen down the drain?
Perhaps you're a ring bearer
in a wedding and you have
no ring to bear? If you're
a witch in need of a ring,
then the Ring Replacer
is the spell for you!*

Henry pumped his fist. "I'm SAVED!" he cried.

"You're not saved yet," said Heidi as she looked at her clock radio. "The wedding starts in thirty minutes."

Heidi read the spell ingredients and directions out loud. "One paper clip, one teaspoon of sugar, one rhinestone. Mix the ingredients together in a bowl. Hold your Witches of Westwick medallion in one hand. Place your other hand over the mix and chant the following words: 'Razzle-dazzle, bling, bling,

bling—turn this mix into a ring!'"

Heidi put down the *Book of Spells*.

"Get a paper clip from my desk," said Heidi.

"Okay," said Henry.

"I'm going to get the sugar and the rhinestone. Be right back!"

Heidi raced downstairs. She quickly
measured a teaspoon of sugar and
placed it in a small bowl. Then she
ran back to her room and opened
her dresser drawer. She pulled out

her DANCE DIVA T-shirt and picked off a pink rhinestone. Then she dropped the rhinestone into the bowl.

Henry added the paper clip.

"We're all ready," said Heidi.

She slipped the medallion around her neck and held it in one hand. She placed her other hand over the mix and chanted the spell. Heidi uncovered the bowl, and they both looked inside. A ring with a huge pink stone in a clawlike setting sat at the bottom of the bowl. Heidi picked it up.

"Whoa," she said. "It's big."

"And bold," added Henry.

"And all wrong," declared Heidi. "It doesn't look anything like Aunt Sophie's wedding ring."

"NOW what are we going to do?" asked Henry.

"There's only one thing left TO do," Heidi said.

"What?" Henry asked.

"Fess up," said Heidi.

Chapter 8

THE REAL THING

Heidi pushed Henry into his bedroom. She watched from the door to see what would happen. Uncle Ned smiled at Henry and did a deep knee bend in his tuxedo. Dad tied his bow tie.

"Ready to roll?" asked Dad. "We

have to be in our places in fifteen minutes."

Henry stood still in front of Dad.

"Is something the matter?" asked Dad.

Henry looked at the floor. "Well, sort of," he began. "It's about Aunt Sophie's ring."

"The ring!" exclaimed Dad. "I almost forgot." Then he reached into his pocket and pulled out Aunt Sophie's ring!

Henry's jaw dropped. "Where did you find it?"

"Nowhere," said Dad. "I've had it all along."

Henry blinked in disbelief. "You didn't think I'd give you the *real* ring?" asked Dad with a wink.

"It wasn't real?" Henry asked.

"No," said Dad. "It was just for practice. Now let's get your ring pillow ready."

Henry grabbed the ring pillow from on top of his dresser. Then Dad snapped the ring in place. Uncle Ned

attached his wedding band beside it.

"Can you take care of the *real* rings until we exchange vows?" asked Uncle Ned.

"Definitely!" said Henry. "And I promise not to take my eyes off them!"

"Great! Then let's have ourselves a wedding!" said Dad.

Chapter 9

A LITTLE PRINCESS

Heidi stepped into the backyard and gasped. At one end of the yard stood a white garden archway swirled with pale pink roses. White folding chairs had been set up in rows in front of the archway, with a path down the middle.

Two of Heidi's cousins played guitars as the guests took their seats. On another side of the yard were tables decorated with white linens, daisies, and votive candles. White paper lanterns had been strung from the tree branches. Next to the tables was a great white tent with tables, a dance floor, and a live band.

Wow, thought Heidi. *This looks like something out of a fairy tale!* Then it dawned on her. *That must be why I'm dressed like a princess!* Heidi felt a tingle of wedding magic.

"Here," said Mom, handing Heidi her flower girl basket.

Heidi lifted the basket to her nose. *Mmm,* she thought. *The roses smell so sweet!* Then she took her place next to Henry, who held his ring pillow proudly.

When the guests had all been seated, the wedding music began. Henry went down the aisle first.

"Good luck!" Heidi whispered.

"You too!" Henry whispered back before walking down the aisle.

Heidi followed behind Henry. She felt beautiful as she tossed the petals all along the aisle. All the guests smiled at Heidi, and she smiled back. *Being in the spotlight isn't so bad,* Heidi thought. Then the wedding

march began. Aunt Sophie walked
down the aisle. She held a bouquet of
freshly cut white roses in her hands.
She took her place next to Uncle Ned.

The bride and groom exchanged
wedding vows and rings. Then they
kissed.

"Eww!" Henry said a little too
loudly.

Everyone laughed and clapped for
the bride and groom.

Then the party began. Heidi and Henry danced on the lawn. They ate grilled chicken, hamburgers, and a double-fudge cake with vanilla cream-cheese frosting. Everyone laughed and clapped again when Henry caught the bride's bouquet.

Later on Heidi and Henry blew
bubbles at Aunt Sophie and Uncle
Ned as they left for their honeymoon.

Heidi sighed dreamily. "I love
weddings," she said.

"What?" questioned Henry. "But I
thought you HATED weddings."

"Not anymore," said Heidi.

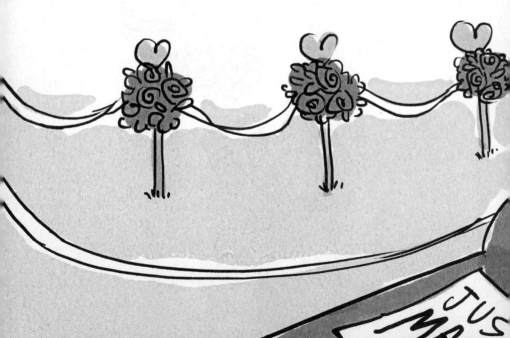

Chapter 10

HARVEST MOON

The next day Heidi and Aunt Trudy went to Harvest Moon to buy some ingredients for Aunt Trudy's brews. Harvest Moon had regular grocery store items, but they also sold hard-to-find products that witches used in brews. Heidi got a shopping cart and steered it into the store.

"So, how did you like being a flower girl?" asked Aunt Trudy as she pulled out her shopping list.

"It was so much better than I thought," Heidi said. "I actually had a great time."

"Wow," said Aunt Trudy. "What changed your thinking?"

Heidi shrugged. "I  dunno," she said. "It was different from what I expected."

"How so?" asked Aunt Trudy.

"Well, I thought it was going to be embarrassing to wear a fancy dress and

walk down the aisle in front of that many people. But it wasn't. It was completely magical."

Aunt Trudy smiled.

"I thought it was magical too. I'm so glad you had a good time."

"Me too," agreed Heidi. "I had the wrong idea about flower girls."

"Well, sometimes things are not always what we expect," Aunt Trudy said.

"No kidding," said Heidi.

They high-fived. Then Aunt Trudy
pulled a jar of bee pollen from the
shelf and placed it into the cart. She
checked her list.

"Heidi, would you find the bay
leaves?" she asked. "I'll get the
pickled ginger. Then we can meet at
the checkout line."

"Sure," said Heidi.

Heidi walked down a few rows and found the spice aisle. When she was partway down she saw a man duck around the corner into the next aisle.

He was bald except for a tuft of hair above each ear.

Hey! thought Heidi. *Is that Principal Pennypacker?* She ran down the aisle and peeked around the corner. But when she looked, he was gone. *That's weird. It must've just been my imagination.*

Or was it?

CONTENTS

SNiFFLES

Ah-choo! sneezed Heidi. *Ah-choo! Ah-choo!*

"Wow, you sure are sneezy today," said Heidi's friend Bruce Bickerson.

Heidi sniffled and smiled. "It's nothing," she said. "Let's finish our leaf pile."

Heidi and Bruce raked the leaves into a colorful mound.

"You go first," Heidi said.

Bruce scurried to the edge of the yard to get a running start. His dog, Frankie, followed close behind.

"One, two, three . . . GO!" shouted Heidi.

Bruce took off, and so did Frankie. It had become a race! Then, *whump!* Frankie disappeared into the leaf pile.

"We have a winner!" cried Heidi.

"Hey, that didn't count!" said Bruce. "Frankie wasn't supposed to race me."

Heidi covered her mouth to keep from laughing. "Okay, do-over!" she said.

They raked another pile of leaves. Then Bruce put Frankie in his dog run so he wouldn't interfere.

"Ready?" called Heidi.

Bruce got into position and gave the ready signal.

"On your mark!" shouted Heidi. "Get set! GO!"

Bruce ran across the yard and

pounced into the leaves. Then he shook off the leaves and ran back to Heidi.

"Your turn!" he said.

Heidi rubbed her forehead.

"What's the matter?" asked Bruce.

"Nothing," Heidi said. "I'm just a little tired."

"Let's get a snack," said Bruce.

"No, thanks," Heidi said, setting down her rake. "I think I'd better get home."

ZONKED

Heidi plopped onto the sofa.

"Dinner's ready," said Mom.

Heidi didn't answer.

"Feel like a taco?" asked Dad.

Heidi loved tacos.

"Nah," she said. "I'm not very hungry."

"Are you sick or something?" asked Henry.

"No-o-o," moaned Heidi.

"Well, you better not be, or you'll miss the Fall Festival," her brother said.

Every year the town of Brewster held a Fall Festival at Thompson's

Homestead. They had scarecrows, pumpkins, a haunted barn, a petting zoo, a hay-bale maze, face-painting, bounce houses, hayrides, and lots of carnival games with prizes. Heidi especially liked the haunted barn. This year Heidi and her best friend, Lucy Lancaster, planned to go through the haunted barn together.

"I'm FINE," Heidi said.

Then she felt a tickle in her nose.

Ah-choo! she sneezed. *Ah-choo!*
Ah-choo!

"Uh-oh," Henry said.

"What?" said Heidi.

"You don't sound very good."

"I just need some orange juice," Heidi said, sitting up.

Heidi forced down a glass of orange juice, but it didn't make her feel any better. Then she made an Aunt Trudy Special: half a cup of honey and half a cup of apple cider vinegar. It smelled awful. But there was no way she was going to miss the Fall Festival. She plugged her nose and drank it down.

"Yuck," she said.

"How about some chicken soup?"
Dad suggested.

"Maybe later," said Heidi.

"How about a good night's rest?" Mom said. "Maybe you'll feel better in the morning."

Rest sounded unexpectedly good. Heidi dragged herself off the couch and plodded upstairs. Mom helped

her into her favorite blue polka-dot
pajamas. Then Heidi crawled right
into bed.

And *zonk*, she was out.

Chapter 3

GROUCHY

I feel horrible, thought Heidi when she woke up. Her throat hurt and her head was stuffed up. She pulled the covers over her face and groaned. Then she yanked the covers right back down. *No!* she told herself. *I have to get up! Today I'm going to help Aunt Trudy set up her booth for the Fall Festival.* Heidi slid out from under the warm covers and plunked her feet on the floor. She rubbed her eyes with the backs of her fists and snuffed up the gook in her nose.

Then she shuffled to the bathroom, splashed cold water on her face, and looked in the mirror.

"You can do this," Heidi said to herself.

She straggled to her bedroom and

sluggishly put on her jeans, a white daisy T-shirt, and a lavender hoodie. She brushed her hair, and headed to the kitchen.

"Well, if it isn't our late sleeper!" said Dad cheerily as he looked up from his bowl of granola.

Heidi sniffled and forced a smile.

Mom closed the lid on the waffle iron

and walked over to Heidi. She put her
hand on Heidi's forehead.

"You're warm," Mom said.

"I'm warm because I just got out of bed," said Heidi as she landed on her chair with a thud.

Mom frowned.

"Ahoy, matey!" shouted Henry, who was sitting in the chair beside her. He was wearing a fake handlebar mustache.

Heidi covered her ears.

Henry shoveled a handful of a waffle into his mouth. Part of his mustache went in with it.

"Want some grub?" asked Henry as he pulled the mustache out of his mouth.

Heidi didn't answer.

Henry picked up his plastic sword and poked his sister in the side.

"Ow!" cried Heidi, yanking the sword from Henry's hand. "Quit it!"

"Well, ex-CUSE me!" said Henry.

Mom placed a waffle and a cup of tea in front of Heidi.

"Mom, Heidi's in a bad mood," Henry said.

"Heidi doesn't feel too well," said Mom.

"I feel FINE," Heidi said.

"You're a grouch," said Henry.

"Leave me alone!" yelled Heidi.

Henry picked up his plate and walked to the sink.

Dad got up and kneeled behind Heidi.

"Maybe you should go back to bed, pumpkin," he suggested.

"No," said Heidi. "I promised Aunt Trudy

I'd help set up her booth for the Fall Festival."

"Aunt Trudy will understand if you don't feel well," said Mom.

Heidi sighed. "But I DO feel well," she lied.

She took a sip of tea and ate a bite of waffle. "See?" she said. "I have a normal appetite and everything!"

Mom and Dad gave each other a worried look.

"I'm good!" Heidi said. "Watch—I'll prove it!"

She jumped up from the table and began to do jumping jacks. She did ten in a row and stopped. Her head throbbed, but she acted like she was okay. "How's that?"

"Not bad," Dad said.

Mom didn't seem so sure, but she went along with it. "Okay, we'll let you help Aunt Trudy," she said. "But if you're not feeling any better, I'm going to bring you straight home."

"I feel GREAT!" said Heidi. Then she ran upstairs to change.

Chapter 4

GERMS!

Heidi and Mom met Aunt Trudy in front of a white canopy tent. Under the tent stood three banquet tables, a bunch of folding chairs, and several boxes of Aunt Trudy's homemade perfumes. She also had two large boxes full of fall decorations and a wheelbarrow filled with pumpkins.

"Let's get started!" said Aunt Trudy as she pulled out three chocolate-brown tablecloths.

Mom and Aunt Trudy unfolded the tablecloths and spread them over all the tables. Heidi rummaged through the decorations and pulled out two scarecrows, a bag full of

colored leaves, and
a stuffed witch
with black-and-
white–striped
stockings. She
hung the scare-
crows on the tent's poles in front of
the booth. Then she set the stuffed
witch on the center table and scat-
tered some of the fall leaves across

the tablecloths. After that she helped her aunt arrange the perfumes on the tables.

Aunt Trudy made perfumes in all kinds of fragrances, like jasmine, cherry blossom, vanilla brown sugar, and peony. She also had some fall fragrances, like pumpkin spice and caramel apple. Heidi liked lily of the valley the best. She squirted some on her wrist and sniffed. She couldn't smell a thing. *Ugh*, she thought. *My nose is too clogged.*

Then Heidi noticed Melanie Maplethorpe standing in front of Aunt Trudy's booth. Melanie had a tray of cider doughnuts in her hands.

"Well, well," said Melanie. "Now I know why it's so STINKY around here!" Then she took one hand off the tray and pinched her nose. "And it's NOT the perfume!"

Heidi tried to ignore Melanie, but

she couldn't. Heidi felt mad *and* sick. She opened her mouth to say something, and then she felt a tingle in her nose.

AH-CHOO! sneezed Heidi.

Melanie looked at her doughnuts.

"EWWW!" she shouted. "You got GERMS all over my doughnuts!"

"I didn't mean to!" cried Heidi.

"Ugh! That is just SO disgusting!" yelled Melanie.

Heidi's mom ran to the rescue.

"Settle down, girls!" she said. "I'll
pay for the doughnuts."

Mom got her wallet and handed
Melanie twenty dollars.

"We're so sorry about your dough-nuts," said Mom. "Heidi has a cold."

Melanie put the money in her jacket pocket and stormed off. She shoved the doughnuts—tray and all—into a trash can. Then she ran back to her booth, where she and her dad were selling doughnuts and muffins.

Mom hugged Heidi. "Don't worry about Smell-a-nie," Mom said. "She'll get over it."

"I doubt it," said Heidi. Then she looked at her mother. "Did you just say SMELL-A-NIE?"

Mom smiled. "You bet I did."

GROUNDED

Heidi lifted a pumpkin from the wheelbarrow and lugged it to the front of the booth. She propped the pumpkin in front of one of the scarecrows. Then she put her hand to her head. *Wow, I feel so tired,* she thought. She sniffled and sat on one of the folding chairs.

"How are you feeling?" asked Mom.

"I just need a little rest," Heidi said.

Mom walked over and felt Heidi's head.

"You're very warm," said Mom. "I'm afraid I'm going to have to take you home."

Aunt Trudy nodded in agreement.

"No-o-o-o!" begged Heidi. "I'll be okay."

"Try to take a little nap," suggested Aunt Trudy, "and come back this afternoon."

Heidi thought about it for a moment. Maybe a nap would do the trick.

"Okay," she said. "But I'm coming right back."

"Good," Aunt Trudy said. "I'll be waiting."

Aunt Trudy gave Heidi a great big hug. Then Heidi and Mom walked to the car. Heidi felt like she was

walking in outer space. She flopped
onto the backseat and shut her eyes.

The next thing Heidi knew, they
were in their driveway. Mom helped
Heidi get to her room. She tucked
Heidi into bed and kissed her on the
forehead.

"Don't forget to wake me up for the festival," mumbled Heidi.

★ ✦ ✳ ◎ ✦

Heidi woke up three hours later. She felt awful, but she rolled out of bed and made her way downstairs to the kitchen. Dad and Henry had their jackets on.

"Where are you going?" asked Heidi in a raspy voice that didn't sound at all like her own.

"They're going to the festival," said Mom. "I called Lucy and told her you wouldn't be able to make it."

Heidi covered her face and began to cry.

"It's okay," Mom said, wrapping her arms around Heidi. "We'll have lots of fun right here. We can make cinnamon spice tea and watch your favorite movie, *The Witch Switch*."

"I'll bring you a treat," promised Henry.

"And I'll try to win a stuffed animal for you," added Dad.

Then they slipped out the back door.

Heidi buried her face in Mom's sweater. She cried until her nose became so stuffy that she couldn't breathe through it. Then she looked at her mom and said, "Why does everything bad happen to me?"

QUiCK FiX

If only I could get rid of this stupid cold, thought Heidi, *then I could go to the festival.* She flopped onto her bed. *It could take days to get better, and by then the festival will be long gone.* Heidi threw her stuffed owl against the wall. It bounced off and rolled

under her dust ruffle. She reached
over to pick it up and noticed her
Book of Spells under the bed. *Wait a
second,* she thought. *Maybe I CAN get
better faster.* She pulled the book out
from under the bed.

"There has to be a spell to cure a
cold," she said to herself.

Heidi looked at the Contents page and found a whole chapter on health. There were remedies for everything from rashes to back pain. Then she found a spell called "No More Sickness!"

"Bingo!" said Heidi as she began to read the spell.

NO MORE SICKNESS!

Do you have an upset stomach? Are you the kind of witch who has a tendency to get tonsillitis? Or perhaps you've just come down with a rotten cold. If anything ails you, then this is the spell for you!

Ingredients:
1 teaspoon of cinnamon
1 cup of peppermint tea
2 tablespoons of ketchup

Mix the ingredients together in a mug. Hold your Witches of Westwick medallion in one hand. Place your other hand over the mix and chant the following words:

SNiFFLE-DEE-DOo!

SNiFFLE-DEE-DAy!

MAk.E THiS SiCKNESS GO AWAY!

Drink the potion and feel your sickness disappear!

The thought of drinking that
mixture of ingredients was totally
disgusting, but it wasn't as bad as
feeling sick. Heidi bookmarked the
page. Then she slid into her fuzzy
blue bunny slippers and headed

downstairs. She paused on the bottom stair and listened. Mom was on the phone. Heidi tiptoed past her office and into the kitchen.

She plopped a tea bag into a mug and filled the mug with warm water. Then Heidi added the cinnamon

and ketchup and stirred
the ingredients together.
When she was done,
she shuffled toward the
stairs with her potion.

"Is that you, Heidi?"
called Mom.

Heidi froze and held her mug close. "Yup, it's me," she said. "I, uh, just wanted some juice."

"Good," said Mom. "Are you up for a movie?"

"I would much rather go to the festival," Heidi said.

"I know, but not this time," Mom said apologetically. "I'll get some pillows and blankets."

Heidi went to her room and shut the door. She sat on the floor and placed her Witches of Westwick medallion around her neck. She held

the medallion in one hand and put her other hand over the mug. Then she chanted the spell. For a moment the mixture bubbled, then it became still again. Heidi took a sip. *It's a good thing I'm too sick to taste this,* she thought. Then she guzzled it down.

Chapter 7

RiBBiT!

Heidi set down the mug and breathed through her nose. The air went right in—just like it was supposed to. *No sniffles!* she thought. Then she swallowed. *No sore throat!* Heidi hopped to her feet and jumped up and down. *I don't have a single ache or pain!* She did a little happy dance. *I feel all better!* she thought. *Now I can go to the festival!*

Heidi couldn't wait to tell her mother. She ran from her room and called to her mom from the top of the stairs.

"RIBBIT!" she shouted. "RIBBIT! RIBBIT!"

Heidi covered her mouth with her hand. *Oh no!* she thought. *I sound just like a frog! Something must've gone wrong!*

Heidi thundered downstairs and ran straight into Mom's office. Mom twirled her chair around.

"What in the world is going on?"
asked Mom. "You sounded like a
herd of buffalo on the stairs. Are you
feeling better?"

Heidi pointed frantically to her
mouth.

Mom looked puzzled. Heidi opened
her mouth and pointed down her
throat.

"You're so silly," she said. "Just tell me if your throat still hurts."

Heidi shook her head and bugged out her eyes. She grabbed a pen from

Mom's pencil cup. Then she peeled off a sticky note and wrote Mom a message:

> I used a spell to get rid of my cold and something went wrong! Now I have a frog in my throat! Help!

Mom read the note and looked at Heidi. "Are you sure?" she asked.

Heidi nodded.

"Try to say something," said Mom.

"RIBBIT!" said Heidi.

"Oh dear!" said Mom.

"RIBBIT! RIBBIT! RIBBIT!" Heidi
said, which translated to "Please help
me!"

Mom put her hands to her cheeks.
"Oh, Heidi!" she said. "You've done it
AGAIN!"

SAY SOMETHING!

Heidi began to cry again.

She peeled off another sticky note and wrote:

Do you think Aunt Trudy can help me?

"She's still at the festival," said Mom. "But don't forget I'm a witch too. Maybe I can figure out what went wrong. Show me the spell you used."

Mom rarely used her witching skills. She tried to live as normal a life as anyone. But today she had to make an exception.

Heidi jotted down another note:

I'll get my book. Be right back!

Heidi ran and got her *Book of Spells*. Then she opened it to the "No More Sickness!" spell. Mom studied the ingredients.

"Hmm," she said. "What kind of tea did you use?"

Heidi answered on a sticky note.

Mint.

"Let's go to the kitchen and have a look," said Mom.

Heidi raced to the kitchen, pulled the tea from the cupboard, and handed it to Mom.

Mom opened the box. She sniffed the tea bags. Then she looked at the label. "Interesting," she said.

"Ribbit?" questioned Heidi, which really meant "What?" in frog. Mom pointed to

the picture on the box. "You used spearmint tea. The recipe calls for peppermint."

Heidi looked puzzled.

"They're different," said Mom. "Spearmint and peppermint are different enough to affect your spell."

Heidi hung her head.

"Now, hold on," said Mom, "and I'll see what I can do."

Mom scurried to her office and came back with her Witches of Westwick medallion. Then she pulled a container of salt and a jar of honey from the cupboard. Heidi sat on a kitchen stool and watched her mom squeeze half a cup of honey into a bowl. Then she added

a teaspoon of
salt and mixed
them together.
Mom spread
the mix on
Heidi's neck

with her fingertips. Then she picked
up her medallion and chanted a spell.

Sha-ZiNG, Sha-ZaNG, Sha-ZoG.
REMOVE THiS CROAKiNG FROG!

Heidi sat and stared at Mom.
"Don't just sit there," said Mom.

"Please say something!"

Heidi tried to think of something clever to say. Then she opened her mouth and went, "OINK! OINK!"

Mom clonked the palm of her hand on her forehead. "Oh no!" she cried. "Now you sound like a pig!"

Heidi smiled.

"Just kidding!" she said.

"Not funny!" said Mom.

"Sorry," Heidi said.

"That's all I could think of to say."

Mom ruffled Heidi's hair.

But there was still one problem.

Chapter 9

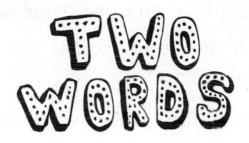

TWO WORDS

Ah-choo! sneezed Heidi. *Ah-choo! Ah-choo!*

She felt completely yucky all over again.

"Sorry, no more fix-it spells," said Mom. "Health cures are too risky. You're just going to have to get well the old-fashioned way."

"Ugh," said Heidi.

"Come on," said Mom. "Let's wash off this honey mixture. Then we can make a nest and watch *The Witch Switch*."

After washing off the sticky mix-ture, Heidi and Mom snuggled on the

couch and watched the movie. It was
dark when Henry and Dad got home.
The boys sat on the couch and tried
to cheer Heidi up.

"I brought you a bag of kettle
corn AND a frosted pumpkin sugar
cookie," said Henry.

"Thanks," said Heidi—even though
she didn't feel like eating anything.

"I got you something too," Dad said.

He pulled a stuffed black cat from behind his back and handed it to Heidi. The cat had an arched back, a frizzed tail, green eyes, and red stitching on its nose and mouth.

"I won it in the football toss," Dad said proudly.

"He had to toss a LOT of footballs,"

Henry whispered.

"I love it," said Heidi, admiring the cat. "What else did you guys do?"

"We went on the hayride," said Henry. "But it was really bumpy. Then we went in the maze."

"And Henry got lost," Dad said.

"I just got a little mixed up," said Henry.

"Did you go in the haunted barn?" asked Heidi.

"Believe it or not, I did!" Henry said.

Henry had never been in the haunted barn before.

"How was it?" asked Heidi.

"Really, really scary," said Henry. "But I loved it!"

Heidi looked at the floor. "I sure wish I could've gone," she said miserably. "The haunted barn is my favorite thing ever. Now I have to wait a WHOLE year until the next one."

Heidi slumped on the sofa and put a pillow over her face.

"Two words," said Henry. "That STINKS."

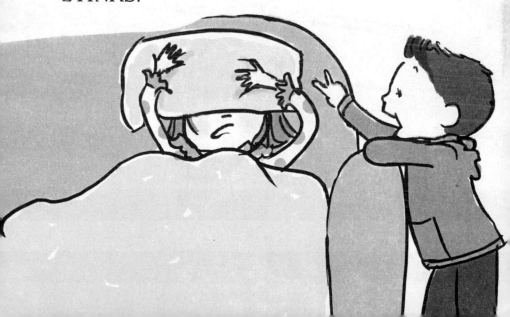

Chapter 10

A SURPRiSE

Heidi missed a whole week of school. By Saturday she felt like her old self.

"Guess what?" said Henry at breakfast.

"What?" asked Heidi.

"Today you're going to get a big surprise!"

"Why?" Heidi asked.

"Because you missed the Fall Festival," said Mom.

"What kind of a surprise?" asked Heidi.

"A haunted house!" said Henry.

Heidi squealed. "I LOVE haunted houses!" she said. "Where is it?"

"In the garage," said Dad.

The Heckelbecks had a big garage. It even had wooden stairs that led to an upstairs storage area.

"It has a real ghost and everything!" said Henry.

"But you have to wait until dark," Mom said.

"Can Lucy come?" asked Heidi.

Mom and Dad looked at each other.

"Lucy had other plans today," said Mom.

"Rats," said Heidi.

"But I still can't wait!"

Heidi and Henry spent the day at Aunt Trudy's. They carved jack-o'-lanterns and made cupcakes with monster faces. After supper Heidi had to wait in her room until her family was ready. At six o'clock her bedroom door creaked open. A hand reached in and turned off the light. Then she

saw Aunt Trudy in the doorway. She had on a jet-black dress with a jagged hem. Her hair had been teased, and she wore smoky eye makeup and bright red lipstick. She held a glowing candelabra in one hand.

"Hello, Heidi," she said in a deeper voice than usual. "My name is Raven, and I'm going to take you to the *haunted* house."

Heidi jumped up and followed

Raven outside and around to the garage. The jack-o'-lanterns had been lit and displayed around the outside. Strands of twinkly orange lights hung from the garage and covered the bushes. A sign on a stake in front of

the garage said FOR SALE, and under-
neath it said DIRT CHEAP.

Raven shook her head sadly.

"I've tried to sell this house for fifty
years, but no one wants to buy it."

"How come?" asked Heidi.

"Are you sure you want to know?" Raven asked.

"Positive," said Heidi.

Raven glanced at the upstairs window of the garage as if she were checking for something. Then she

looked back at Heidi. "This house is haunted," she whispered.

Heidi's eyes grew wide. Even though she knew there were no such things as ghosts, she began to feel a tingle in her spine.

"By what?" questioned Heidi.

"By a *ghost*," Raven whispered.

Raven opened the door to the garage, and a cold, eerie mist swept over Heidi.

They stepped inside, and Raven went on whispering. "No one ever knows when the ghost will appear," she said as she looked uncertainly all around her.

Heidi heard a door creak somewhere in the garage. The inside of the garage had been made to look like rooms in somebody's house.

"Do you think the ghost will come out today?" asked Heidi.

Raven paused for a moment. "We shall soon see," she whispered.

Then Heidi heard someone moan.

"I WANT TO COME DOWN!" said an eerie voice from up the wooden stairs.

"What was that?" asked Heidi, biting the corner of a fingernail.

Raven looked up. "Oh no," she whispered. "I fear it may be the *ghost*!"

A dusty piano then began to play

"Chopsticks" all by itself. Heidi never realized how creepy "Chopsticks" could sound in a dark, spooky garage.

She pointed at the piano. "How is it doing that?"

"The ghost likes to play the piano," said Raven. "But it's funny, it doesn't seem to need to be at the piano to play it."

Then the voice from upstairs

wailed again. "I WANT TO COME
DOWN!" it cried.

"Come," Raven said. "I'd like to
show you the dining room."

Heidi followed Raven into the dining room.

The table was set for dinner. A
mummy sat at one end of the table

and a skeleton at the other. A zombie
boy sat on one side.

"I'm hungry!" said the zombie boy.
"Would you please take the lid off my
dinner?"

Raven nodded to Heidi.

Heidi looked at the domed platter. *Don't be afraid,* she told herself.

Remember, this is all fake. Then she bit her bottom lip, lifted the lid, and screamed.

"*Aaaaaaaaaah!*"

There was a head on the platter, and it waggled its tongue at Heidi! Heidi grabbed on to Raven and held tight.

"Yuck!" complained the zombie

boy. "We had somebody's head for dinner LAST night!"

Heidi took a closer look at the ghoulish head on the platter. It looked an awful lot like Dad.

Then a door banged upstairs.

"I'M COMING DOWN!" said the ghostly voice.

Raven led Heidi into the living room.
Huge spiders hung from the ceiling.
An old lady rocked in a chair with her
knitting. A black cat sat beside her. It
hissed at Heidi. Then the coffin coffee
table in front of the old lady began to
creak. The lid slowly opened, and a

vampire boy rose from inside.

"Good evening . . . ," he said. "I vant to suck your blood!"

Heidi hid behind Raven.

"Oh, don't mind him," said the old lady. "He just wants his bottle."

The old lady handed Heidi a baby bottle full of what looked like blood.

Heidi shut her eyes and handed the bottle to the vampire boy. He slurped it down.

"Thank you," said the vampire boy.
"That vuz vunderful!"

Then the boy lay back down in
the coffin and shut the lid.

"I'M COMING DOWN!" said the spooky voice from upstairs.

The old lady stopped knitting and looked at Heidi.

"Little girl, you must get out of this house!" she warned. "Get out while you can!"

The wailing voice got a little bit louder. "I'M COMING DOWN!"

The dim lights began to flicker.

"We'd better go," urged Raven. She rushed Heidi toward the door.

But it was too late! They ran right

into the ghost on the bottom stair.
The ghost wore a ragged dress and
had a sheet over its face. It hopped
from the stair and landed in front of
Heidi.

"Boo!" said the ghost.

Heidi screamed and ran out the
door and onto the driveway.

"WAIT!" shouted the ghost as she chased Heidi out of the garage. "It's ME, LUCY!"

Heidi turned around. "Lucy? Is that really YOU?"

"Yes!" cried Lucy.

Then everyone came out: Mom, Dad, Henry the zombie, Aunt Trudy,

and the vampire boy, who was really Heidi's friend Bruce.

Heidi began to laugh.

"Did we scare you?" asked Henry.

"Did you EVER!" said Heidi, still catching her breath. "That haunted house was the BEST!"

"Yes!" said Henry, pumping his fist.

Everyone cheered. Then they all went into the Heckelbecks' house and had monster cupcakes and goblets filled with blood . . . which, of course, was really just fruit punch.

Check out the next book starring

Yum!

Yummy!

Yumsicles!

Heidi Heckelbeck loved pizza day. She slid a hot slice of pepperoni pizza onto her lunch tray. Then she sat down with her friends Lucy Lancaster and Bruce Bickerson.

"I have great news!" said Bruce.

An excerpt from *Heidi Heckelbeck Is Not a Thief!*

"What?" asked Heidi and Lucy at the same time.

Bruce looked around to make sure no one was listening. Then he lowered his voice to a whisper. "My latest invention is finished!" he said. "But don't tell anyone. It's top secret!"

Bruce's inventions were always top secret. He didn't want anyone to steal his ideas, but he trusted his two best friends, Heidi and Lucy.

"What's it called?" asked Heidi excitedly.

Bruce leaned forward so only the girls could hear. The girls leaned in too.

An excerpt from *Heidi Heckelbeck Is Not a Thief!*

"I'm calling it the Bicker Picker-Upper," he whispered.

"What does it do?" Lucy asked.

"It picks stuff up *automatically*," said Bruce.

"Like a robot?" asked Heidi.

"Like a robot's arm," Bruce said.

"What kinds of things does it pick up?" asked Lucy.

"Stuffed animals, action figures, socks, underwear, pajamas—basically everything on my floor," said Bruce.

"It picks up your room?" Heidi questioned as she took a big bite of pizza. "THIS I gotta see!"

An excerpt from *Heidi Heckelbeck Is Not a Thief!*

"Me too!" said Lucy.

"Can you guys come over after school tomorrow?" asked Bruce.

"Probably," said Heidi.

"I'll check with my mom," Lucy said. Then she pulled her baby owl notepad from her backpack.

Lucy also took out a pink pen shaped like a lollipop. The lollipop had a spiral design and sparkled with pink and silver glitter. She wrote a reminder on her notepad:

ASK permission to go to Bruce's house tomorrow.

An excerpt from *Heidi Heckelbeck Is Not a Thief!*

The lollipop lit up as she wrote. Heidi dropped her pizza on her lunch tray and stared at Lucy's pen.

"WHERE did you get THAT?" asked Heidi.

Lucy twirled the pen in front of her friends.

"Isn't it beautiful?" she said. "My dad brought it back from his last business trip."

"I LOVE it!" said Heidi. "May I see?"

"Sure!" Lucy said.

But just then the bell rang. It was time to go back to the classroom. Lucy dropped the pen into her backpack.

An excerpt from *Heidi Heckelbeck Is Not a Thief!*

"I'd better show you at recess," she said.

"But I want to see it NOW!" Heidi complained.

Lucy laughed. "I promise I'll show you LATER!"

"Oh, okay," said Heidi.

Then they cleared their trays and headed down the hall.

If you like Heidi Heckelbeck, you'll love
the adventures of
SOPHIE MOUSE